The Mare on the Hill

THE MARE ON THE HILL

by Thomas Locker

A Puffin Pied Piper

PUFFIN PIED PIPER BOOKS
Published by the Penguin Group
Penguin Books USA Inc., 375 Hudson Street, New York, New York, 10014, U.S.A.
Penguin Books Ltd, 27 Wrights Lane, London W8 5TZ, England
Penguin Books Australia Ltd, Ringwood, Victoria, Australia
Penguin Books Canada Ltd, 10 Alcorn Avenue, Toronto, Ontario, Canada M4V 3B2
Penguin Books (N.Z.) Ltd, 182–190 Wairau Road, Auckland 10, New Zealand
Penguin Books Ltd, Registered Offices: Harmondsworth, Middlesex, England

Originally published in hardcover by Dial Books
A Division of Penguin Books USA Inc.

Library of Congress Catalog Card Number: 85-1684
Printed in the U.S.A.
First Puffin Pied Piper Printing 1995
ISBN 0-14-055339-8
3 5 7 9 10 8 6 4 2

A Pied Piper Book is a registered trademark of Dial Books,
a division of Penguin Books USA Inc.,
® TM 1,163,686 and ® TM 1,054,312.

THE MARE ON THE HILL is also available in hardcover from
Dial Books.
The art for each picture consists of an alkyd and oil painting.

To Maria and the boys

It was spring when we first saw the white mare. Grandpa had gone to a horse sale to buy a mate for our stallion. Late in the day he returned leading a beautiful white mare. My brother Aaron and I ran to meet him.

Grandpa had told us that the mare had been mistreated by her first owner. She was afraid of people and would have to be tied up. Aaron and I didn't want that. We pleaded with Grandpa to set the mare free.

"You'll never be able to catch her," he warned. But he took the mare's halter off and let us open the pasture gate.

With a frightened whinny she bolted into the pasture and galloped away. Our stallion ran after her, but the mare didn't stop until she got to the top of the hill.

On the hill, far away from people, the mare seemed to feel safe. There was plenty of grass for her to eat, a pool of spring water, and a grove of sheltering trees. Aaron and I watched the mare and the stallion all summer long as the grass grew tall and the hot weather came.

Nearly every day we walked up the hill and tried to catch the mare. But Grandpa had been right. Each time she saw us, she ran away. We never even came close. Summer ended and in September Aaron and I went back to school. I guess our dog was lonely because she went up the hill then and made friends with the mare.

Autumn came. The leaves on the trees changed color and apples ripened in the orchard. Each day after school Aaron and I carried apples to the mare. We left them near the spring, hoping she would come to us, but she never did. One day Aaron said he thought the mare was pregnant.

"She is not!" I told him. But when we asked Grandpa, he said it was true. The mare would have a foal in the spring.

One morning I looked out the window and saw it was snowing. I was worried about the mare. I knew she could dig through the snow to get to the grass, but there was not much grass left. Grandpa told us that she would come down from the hill when she was hungry enough. Aaron and I waited a few days. Then we began to carry hay and oats up to her.

That winter was the coldest in years. Even Grandpa said so. By December it was dark when we came home from school. Day after day Aaron and I struggled through the snowdrifts to take food to the mare. At last she started to wait for us. We left it lower on the hill each time, hoping to lure her down to the barn.

But before this could happen, the weather changed. The snow melted and the barnyard became muddy. It was spring. In the cool April days, while Aaron and I helped with the planting, the mare returned to the hill. Grass had begun to grow in the pasture and she no longer needed our help.

One day while we were in school a storm came roaring down from the mountains. The sky turned black and the trees were swaying in the fierce wind. All I could think about was the mare and how frightened she would be alone on her hilltop. As soon as school was over, I got Aaron and we ran home.

An old tree had fallen across the fence. The pasture was open. Aaron and I searched everywhere, calling to each other above the howling of the wind. Then I thought I heard our dog barking. We raced down the hill to the barn. There, standing placidly beside our stallion, was the white mare.

That was in early May. From then on the mare stayed close to the barnyard. Aaron and I spent hours on the fence, watching her with the stallion and wondering when she would have her foal. One day we brought carrots to the horses. I gave some to the stallion. The mare watched for a time and then she came right up to Aaron and ate a carrot from his hand.

One morning soon afterward Grandpa came into our room and woke us up. "Hurry, come to the pasture behind the barn," he whispered.

Aaron and I knew right away what had happened. We raced to the pasture and there we saw the mare cleaning her newborn foal. As we drew closer, the mare looked up at us. In the soft dawn light she seemed proud and welcoming, and she was calmer than she'd ever been before.